Welcome to
Buss ~~Ask~~, Maryland
ASS!

Wobblestrut

& Other Proclivities

To God, my ancestors, devoted parents,
friends' affirmations, the love of my life,

and the immaculacy of I.

Wobblestrut

& Other Proclivities

Leslie Summerfield

TABLE OF CONTENTS

Outside Soverign

Raised in a village
All minding themselves inside;
Kings are born outside.

Comfortable County
Easy is a pantomime;
Queens run style; Ask.

Don't care what you see,
Lobotomized, gaunt zombie.
Almost home, playa,

Outside Sovereign

What's it like having life chew on you like cud?

I. Lowlife:
The Seed Coronation of L. Apollo

It was sometime in 2015 when thirty-something Lennie Apollo, debonair in the prime of his life peddling fancy furniture for a decade, asked for a raise to start a family. The company, named after cheap shipping material, promptly responded a fortnight later to decline with a month's severance.

"Ya asked for a shilling and got the boot," a canary sang to the handsome young man with a close cut and fresh shape-up as cheap beer lifted his poor spirits on a sunlit wooden back porch overlooking his manicured lawn out in the County.

His tears were masked behind endless quips and heroic retellings to the bird of what they called being "let go"—which was bullshit, by the way.

He was FIRED, and he wouldn't be sitting at home if he hadn't dared ask for eleven percent; which only reflected a fraction of what he brought in. And, of course, his efforts continued to generate even more revenue for the firm. But now, they didn't have to split any of it with Lennie.

Then again, this happened to people all the time—from truly nobody's fault at all. Lennie's ambition could've looked arrogant as he underestimated his leverage. Perhaps it was only a matter of time before this would've happened to him anyway; maybe getting canned saved someone else's livelihood.

Still, he'd miss his colleagues like Hester and Chase. But it wouldn't be long before he heard from them less—then barely—before becoming familiar strangers to one another; no longer worshipping the same HR deity. A shame, he'd later quip to himself; he found them weird, gifted, and a bit fun.

"Why don't ya sit for a few weeks, just to figure out what ya wanna get into next?" the bird mused before shitting on Lennie's shoulder and flying away.

Watching the guano spool down his maroon shirt like melted vanilla ice cream was the last thing holding Lennie back before tears flooded from his ducts, pouring down his dark-almond, sun-kissed cheek and onto his pressed black slacks. The gut punch of failure, sudden position of destitution, and prospect of getting out of a mess he created for himself all washed away for a moment with that gentle permission to be nothing for a bit.

Nonetheless, Lennie couldn't sit still for the foreseeable future inside and outside his Maryland suburban-tucked rancher with a spacious basement. All he could utter was a mumble as the first of many cracks hissed from a clear-glassed bottle with a long neck.

"COUCH-SLUMPED HIGHLIFE FOR A LOWLIFE,"

Lennie said with the chuckle of a bum as he gulped down the American lager.

He was fired, or let go, or whatever the fuck, on a Tuesday, so the following Wednesday morning was jarring, to say the least. It was a cool feeling, like he had the day off; except it was indefinite, and he wasn't welcomed back. By noon, his years of career and dedication crumbled into destitution, hitting him worse than the concussion he got after falling off a golf cart when he was a kid. His living room became an encampment: the grey couch ran dating show reruns while a throw pillow was damp and muffled.

Lennie's spoiled cats could only describe what came out of his mouth as desperate wailings of rejection. Their helpless human looked even more pitiful than he usually did, but both the black and grey nepeta-turnt felines heard something, barely audible, leaving Lennie's mouth and heart before he fell into something reminiscent of an overdose. Or coma.

"Thank you, and I'm sorry."

The countless highs for the lowlife and goofy gummy bears for his grumbling tummy disassociated the anointed man from what was and wasn't, what could and what should, for about five hours.

During that time, everything was a black blur to Lennie. The last thing he remembered, his cats were chasing each other around the house as people spitting on another played on the television. Looking around the devoid depths of himself, he imagined death could be something like this.

Maybe he accidentally killed himself while coping on the couch. Lennie tried to panic at the thought but felt an immediate sense of relief that, if true, he was cool with parting from the world of living that seemingly had enough of him.

Lennie began to smile at his imagined misfortune. Then, a warm, veiny, and callused hand slapped him to the ground.

Looking up and rubbing his cheek, Lennie saw himself, but different. He was definitely older, but he couldn't tell by how much, as black doesn't crack. His older self was dressed in breezy linen pants and a button-up shirt covered in eccentric, Afrocentric designs with several buttons undone at the top.

To the recently cast away Lennie, this version was undoubtedly cooler, calmer, more collected—better. His thick Cuban Linx gold chain hung around his neck and down to his chest, with a matching bracelet on one wrist. Lennie read Armani on the man's watch and noticed why his face was hurting from that slap—there was a massive ring on his older self's pinky finger, next to a wedding band. In all, Lennie couldn't deny the exponential accomplishment and success this man possessed, compared to what Lennie had stripped from him, even with dirty-ass crocs on.

The younger Lennie only felt pity for himself, a neutered lion. But before the despair could pull him from the land of living into the torturous toybox of

Tartarus, the older yet unmistakably baller vestige of himself put his hand on Lennie and grinned, revealing a glistening gold tooth.

"I'm not better than you if you have to make me first," the older Lennie said, looking him in the eyes.

Lennie tried to ask him who he was, why he was here, and what he was supposed to do, but the man interrupted him with a burp and sported another grin.

"You'll live the answer," the man said before dissipating into a plume of smoke or vape—Lennie couldn't tell which.

When Lennie woke up gargling in his own drool, he found his cats looking at him in bewilderment. Surprisingly, he felt nothing towards the career he held dear and integral to his future. Or to the idea that it would give him everything he needed to be happy. To Lennie, that place became no different from any gig he'd had in the past: stifling, underpaid, and riddled with exploit.

Nobody, no employer, would put him in this position ever again. It wasn't an empty threat; that thought, feeling, and idea was no different to him than understanding he needed to drink water, eat bread, or breathe clean air.

More importantly, Lennie realized there was something his older self didn't have. In hindsight, it was clear that the man of mystery didn't give a fuck about what anyone said to him. It was a frightening thought. If Lennie wanted to be treated well, he needed to treat people well, too, right?

Enough with that bullshit, Lennie immediately thought to himself.

Look where that had got him: a chump he vowed to never become again.

But to achieve that, Lennie knew he had to make himself—that was what his striking older self said. And now, with his greatest challenge for fulfillment and happiness understood, Lennie began practicing a grin in the bathroom mirror that revealed a dimple he seemingly always had.

Days later as Lennie cleaned his basement, he came across an old bass his father gave him twenty years ago that collected dust and fingernail shrapnel. When he was a youngster, he took lessons, knew a few scales by heart, played with fellow pupils, and knew basslines to some of his favorite songs.

But reality television, MMORPGs, beer, ladies, and anxiety soon riddled Lennie, with his gifts on the strings vanishing. He'd always lament it!

Taking a cloth to the guitar, he wiped it clean and then plugged it into the same amp he remembered his dad lugging to some fancy Italian restaurant on his twelfth birthday. Lennie thought for a moment about being unemployed but then curled his lip before strumming the bass guitar with one hand, his other choking its neck. Like a little ditty, Lennie played a scale without effort.

He later found the tuner in a storage box during one of his daily afternoon practices.

Another time during his weeks of nothingness, Lennie was again in the basement. This time, he wore only his True Religion briefs, steel-toed boots, and an Ocean City beach towel tied around his head like a bandana. He looked at himself in front of a flimsy mirror from Walmart, alternating between bicep curls with twenty-pound dumbbells and guttural huffs with each controlled movement.

Only Lennie's girlfriend of many years and his closest friends knew, with incredulous amusement, how he preferred working out like this—as he claimed he looked amazing doing it.

Plus, it took too long to get dressed just to get sweaty. "Cut the middleman," he always said.

After one rep, he noticed how far his grin had come along, dimple sparkling in the low light. Lennie was never an athletic man, only staying toned to impress the divine feminine. Now, it was to make sure his body's as fit as his mind was becoming.

Though adulation was always welcome, it was more like a cherry on top for the man. Lennie reminded himself of this as he watched the towel soak the sweat from his nappying head, body fat burning away his shame.

After the eleventh rep on each arm, Lennie smirked at how vascular his arms were getting.

Still, when Lennie ran out of steam, needed rest, or could do nothing but be nothing, he found himself humming his hymn.

There was one night on his back porch, when Lennie downed a Highlife in one gulp as he stared at a yellow moon that reminded him of a rich custard. He continued to gaze with a wobbly posture; not from the alcohol by volume —maybe certainly so—but because he hadn't found the answer yet. On how to make himself. Playing bass, getting fit for the right reasons, those were crucial for him to get back to himself, to make himself.

But they weren't the answer he was looking for, and sitting for weeks was starting to weigh him down as the core belief for his destiny was somewhere among the stars.

His parents unwittingly raised him both a prophet and the captain of his own ship; and he accepted right then on his porch just how comfortable he became, which could be considered a loser's life to some. All he needed to do right now was fit into his king.

Weeks later, that last piece would come during a routine trip to the hardware store and change everything.

That said, it wasn't long before Lennie Apollo finally graduated from lowlife back to being a contributing member of society. Thanks to some amazing changes in Maryland, Lennie accepted an opportunity to market an interesting flower and its derivatives. But by this time, Lennie Apollo had a completely different air to himself, his grown-out, curly black hair bouncing in parallel.

Using his first bonus, Lennie bought three quarters of an acre of raw land on the shitty side of Buss Ask. Within a year, his new and unwittingly declared idiot W-2 paid for boundary surveying, permits, and tree mulching as Lennie arranged for a discarded shipping container to be placed on the raw plot. He and some persuaded cohorts spent season after season clearing and fencing the property and strangely, as the years passed and his life unfolded, Lennie Apollo's answer unfolded as if it had a mind of its own.

Laying out on his lawn and looking up at the sky with a joint hanging out his mouth, Lennie found himself returning, that was for sure. But there was still work to be done, and time to pass.

The bags under his eyes didn't show it, but Lennie could see it now. Looking at the calluses forming on one hand before taking a drag and blowing a puff of smoke into the air like a dragon, he estimated it wouldn't be long before he blew his tithe in libations to his uncle and idols with old buddies. His kids would be spoiled-gifted, with everyone he cared about eating good. Most importantly, anyone who helped this crazy shit take off could have the same kind of things he wanted. Home, family, hobbies, and investments.

Forty hours should give that, and negotiating for anything less should be sin, Lennie began internalizing.

A mule with forty acres would be a start, he'd quip right after.

Lennie wanted to amass a wealth, legacy, and wisdom that only heirs could understand. Who else could he trust with what he wanted to build and be the standard bearer of it?

While he was at it, still completely sprawled across not even a percent of his lawn, he realized the County was becoming too small for him. He loved his home and never imagined leaving it for good. But the man who always hated to travel was strangely excited for other good-looking people across the globe to witness his greatness. And vice versa.

Still, baggermen collected forty or fifty-something-plus clanking glass bottles on Monday's recycling route as the years passed slower than White Owl white grapes, with everyone riding life's turbulent magnet train out of their control.

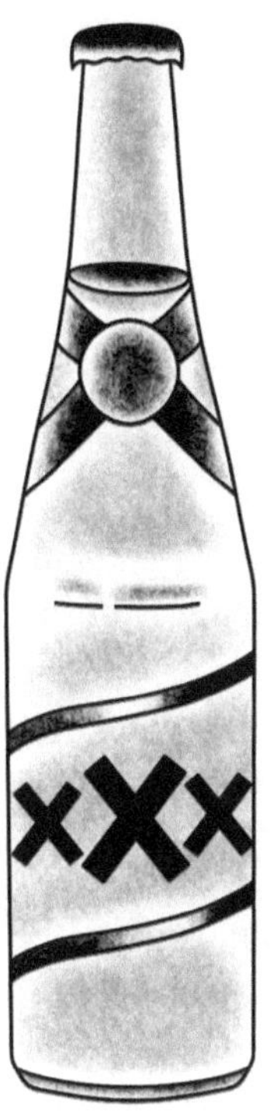

FIGLI DI EROS

There's an old uncles' tale going around Buss Ask, orated across generations.

They say each person is born to one of the four primordial Forces.

The Harbinger of Chaos allows everything and all to emerge from its endlessness. Gaia of the Earth molds the land, sea, and sky for life to thrive. Meanwhile, all Tartarus, Warden of the Underworld, cares for is hoarding the never-ending influx of dearly departed.

But the fourth, Eros, is different from its siblings.

While complimenting the others in helping or harming humanity, Eros repels the other Forces, like a magnet with an opposing pole. Yet at the same time, it acts as an invisible jumper cable, sparking emotion from even a speck of ordinary. Embodying the masculine and feminine, indiscriminately striking with the sudden force of a dumpster truck, Eros brings together all things—from matter, to Gods, to mankind itself.

Maybe humans are the hardest for Eros, Attraction's Pull, to pair together. Then again, not a day's gone by in recorded history with zero roads built, weddings officiated, birth certificates signed, or wars meeting unnecessary soldier with unnecessary soldier.

Not to mention, not a single day has passed where two people didn't shake hands for the first time, overcome mutual challenges, chat over lunch, pursue curiosity about each other; or share a kiss—a bed.

One could argue we're not just the easiest for Eros to entice; we're limerent-ridden slaves to this great magnetic Force.

The Children of Eros, if you will.

"I'm walking up to the restaurant now," says a young man on the phone. "It's 7:02 right now, so you'll only be a little late."

"Fine, text me when you're walking up," he says, making sure not to trip on a curb.

"You love me?" he asks the woman on the other line. "Yeah, you too. See you soon."

He ends the call.

Approaching the manicured entrance to a rustic establishment, 28-year-old Reese Marathon is perplexed that his coworkers chose this place for dinner and drinks—Figli di Eros. Only because it's out in the County instead of somewhere nice near their office in Buss Ask's business district. Still, walking up to the restaurant, you can tell it's fancy from just the outside. To Reese, the building looks like it was built entirely in the Italian countryside and then dropped onto the County's lakeside mall front. Reese can only imagine how many anniversaries, birthdays, and engagements take place at this restaurant daily.

Like it oozes occasion, romance, and high prices.

Nonetheless, it brings warmth to his face in the February cold, as the restaurant is tucked away right next to the mall he grew up near. On this Saturday evening, days after Valentine's, the memories flood him: scouring through the mall's 1970s architecture with his grade school friends, just twenty dollars to his name and an 8:45 p.m. movie to make in time.

That was all before high school warehouse parties and hanging asses out the windows of beat-up minivans. Reese lets the memories fade, as he's now fresh into a new decade and hears his 2019 Tesla beep, letting its owner of one year know that the red EV of innovation is locked safe.

The comfort of being near where he grew up suddenly makes Reese grit his recently whitened teeth. He's trying to convince himself that being this close to home won't affect the evening since he's chopping it up with some friends from his job.

According to its website, Pallet is one of the top furniture wholesalers in the National Capital Region—the biggest, really, with warehouses, offices, and goods in every major big-box store across the DMV.

He and these two guys usually grab beers or check out something fun after work around Buss Ask—and the shittier part they call Buss Ass. They've even introduced Reese to their partners on occasion.

And tonight's the night they finally get to meet

Casey. His Casey. The thought makes Reese nervous.

He hopes they like her.

At that moment, a ping gives a brief rumble to the mid-level data entry analyst's pocket. He just got off the phone with her—his imperfect yet faithful, smart, and trying partner of many months—who's running a few minutes late. Coming straight from her job in the capital, she'd call if something came up.

So if it wasn't Casey texting him, then Reese has an idea who's on the other end. The fabric from his slacks rubs against his teak-toned hand as he retrieves the phone from his pocket and opens the message:

Rebecca: Have fun at the Pallet happy hour! (loser)

Reese smiles at the message from his fellow sledge in the bullpen, Rebecca the antique appraiser. Wanting to answer with something snarky, he shoots back a playful reply in seconds—still smiling.

Reese: I'll try, have fun being anti-social haha

She hearts the message.

The people he's meeting tonight are cool and all, but Reese admits to himself that Rebecca's the person he feels most comfortable with at work. Known around the office for her platinum pigtails, green eyes, and always traveling somewhere cool, she's one of the first people Reese actually shook hands with when he started at Pallet. She's also the one he talks with the most, since they work alongside each other in the same bullpen for the entry- and mid-levelers.

It's only been a bit past six months since he started, but he and Becca have shared a bunch with each other while their fingers tapped endless characters on their keyboard. And during lunch at their desks. Things like where they both grew up, where they got their degrees, and what dumb issues they were dealing with as post-graduates and young professionals.

You know, usual stuff.

Just a step from entering the restaurant, Reese appraises himself in the glass door's reflection, next to a campaign flier taped at eye level that reads (R) COTEY RICCI FOR SENATOR 2020. Reese is wearing his sharpest suit—fitting as fuck and all black—and only wears it to job interviews, church services, weddings, or funerals. Any big event, for that matter.

Combing his slicked-back, black hair with his fingers, he reties his red, snakeskin dress shoes and makes sure his thin beard is still symmetrical before entering.

Walking through the large swinging doors, Reese expects the restaurant's interior to be like any other Italian joint that he's been to throughout his life and for his own anniversaries. But instead, the up-and-coming young man is met with an intimate setting grander and fancier than he imagined.

This establishment would take the bougiest gourmand's breath away. From the outside, Reese expected a knock-off, yet more expensive Olive Garden. Instead, he finds stone pillars towering over him, upscale patrons seated in sleek black leather furniture, with crystal dishware neatly placed at each table. Lining the walls are old Italian photographs, fancy artwork from who knows when, and newspaper clippings on Mussolini facing his comeuppance.

Reese notices a glass display stacked with culinary awards, even older art, and what appears to be a photograph of the restaurant's owner and his little brother, the man running for senator. Both men look alike—somewhere in their thirties, with white-almond skin and ash-brown curls. Several years older than Reese, the restaurant's owner is in traditional chef's whites, holding a plate of bolognese to the camera. His brother, Cotey, gives a cheesy, thumbs-up endorsement to the dish.

Passing the display, Reese approaches reception, where a marble statue easily fifteen feet tall overlooks the dining and bar section. Assuming it's some half-naked Greek dude, or maybe a Roman god from centuries ago, Reese crooks his neck at the statue; noticing it has large breasts and an even bigger cock. Nonetheless, he finds it an immaculate sculpture, with long, thick, swirly hair going down its back. To Reese, the statue stands like a sentinel of sensuality over the restaurant.

He's yet to find his table, and already feels confident that this could be the best Italian restaurant he's ever patronized.

He's about to snap a quick photo of the endowed statue in its loosely hanging robes when he feels the ping's buzz in his hand. Fingers doing what the eyes want to see, Reese scans the message before double-tapping it on his phone, delivering a small, red-hearted emoji.

Rebecca: Shut up, you're just the only

cool person in the office!

Reese's thoughts make a sharp pivot to Casey. She shouldn't be too long, he thinks to himself. He reaches the podium-like, white, marble counter that displays delicious refrigerated Italian desserts, and a receptionist who couldn't be older than twenty greets him.

"Hi! Welcome to Figli di Eros!"

Reese takes in her espresso-toned skin and smoldering, hazelnut eyes and jokes silently that she must have come with the building from a Sardinian countryside.

"Do you have a reservation?" she asks.

"I do, party of six for 7:00 p.m.," Reese says. "The name on the reservation might be under Pal—"

"REESE!" yells a familiar voice. "Over here!"

The busty and big-dicked statue witnesses Reese scan a few tables in the dining section before he spots Hester, Pallet's graphic designer. With bright red hair and an even brighter bejeweled jumpsuit, 30-year-old Hester with parents from Sri Lanka waves Reese over with his dusky-toned hands, fitted with rhinestone rings on all ten fingers.

The statue—with guests always too busy with their meals, drinks, and conversation to notice—takes note of the four people at the table. Two seats remain empty, reserved for Reese and Casey.

Next to Hester is his fiancé, Luciana. A short and jubilant woman from Spain similar in age to her partner, Reese remembers how much trouble she had viewing the stage when she once joined them for a concert.

The guy next to them is Chase, Pallet's underwriter from Boston. His wavy blonde hair and blue eyes remind Reese—and even the statue—of a retired, lax bro in his early thirties who's done a good job of not turning into a racist asshole, even though The Wolf of Wall Street is one of his favorite movies.

Reese can only imagine how the woman beside Chase, his wife Maude, reins him in at home. The statue knows, and smirks at the thought. A quiet woman from the Eastern Shore, Maude often comes by the office with their young children to have lunch with her husband.

The statue raises its eyebrow as it notices Reese thinking to himself to always "save the best for last."—meaning himself. It's amused by the man's flawed logic that being the last to arrive at events somehow adds to his reputation as one of the cooler guys around the office.

"He's arrived!" says Chase, laughing. "We almost ordered without you!"

"Hey, everyone," Reese says, the statue still amused by how suave and secure the man thinks he is.

"Where's Casey?" Maude asks, looking behind Reese. "I can't wait to meet her!"

"Me too!" Luciana chimes in, playfully eyerolling at the man.

"She should only be a few more minutes," Reese says, a bead of sweat falling down his neck. "Coming from D.C."

"She's a literary agent, right?" Hester asks. "You mention her so much, it'll be cool to meet the legend herself."

As Reese sits down at the table, his lap buzzes with a quick ping. He briefly pulls out his phone and sees the message from Rebecca. It's a link to a song from Spotify, probably the fifth that she's shared with him this week.

"Yeah, she's really excited to meet you all, too," says Reese with a quiet titter, putting his phone back into his pocket after hearting Rebecca's text.

The statue notices how Reese's laughter is half-hearted and riddled with mock modesty. He's never meant half of what he's shared about Casey's gifts and their life together, even if it's all factually accurate. To him, talking his partner up makes her look good, which makes him look even better.

"At Figli di Eros, each party, no matter the size, is given a pair of servers," Luciana says, noticing Reese's surprise at a waitress and waiter approaching their table seconds later.

"Apparently, it's to achieve what they call the most attentive service known to fine dining," Hester adds.

The statue is tickled at how diligent the pair is on researching establishments before patronizing them.

Everyone orders high spirits, with Reese ordering one for Casey as well.

"I hope they won't take long," Chase says, looking around with a finger tapping on the table.

Teased around the office for his impatience with long lines, Chase's fear is warranted from the sheer volume of tables, patrons, and endless orders around them. Which is why the statue's nipples twitch at the five's awe when their first round of hand-crafted drinks arrives mere minutes later.

Chatting over drinks, the statue watches Reese note himself to enjoy the moment. Scarcity is always of high value, he believes. Reese doesn't go out often, but when he does, he likes it just like this. Nobody knows too where he grew up, how much acne he had, how anxious he used to be, and how much of a loser he was then, compared to now.

Marble eyes wander the table as Reese nurses a Penicillin. It's elated to see such young, talented, quirky, and gorgeous people from nearly every corner of the world; here at one table. To the statue, this is like having front row seats to a human performance that even Gods couldn't get tickets to. It continues watching Reese with interest as he holds court so freely, with so much confidence, so much knowledge on the subject matter they're discussing. It can tell it makes Reese feel so large—yet doesn't realize the opposite's more realistic.

Still, his skills and work ethic have earned him enough money to buy a home in the County, with enough spare time to sleep all he wants in his free time. There's even room to take his relationship with Casey to the next level. The statue shakes its head when it sees Reese privately admit they're closer to marriage than ever—something that excites him—but maybe all that can wait until he gets a promotion.

After all, a marriage done wrong, without a plan, sounds immature.

It's during Hester's rant about proper flushing in the office bathroom that Reese texts Rebecca to remember to flush next time. You know, in case he forgets to tell her at work.

Everyone places their second drink order, Casey's Last Word collecting condensation on its glass. Chase coughs loud enough to catch everyone's attention.

"Oh, one thing," Chase says after taking a gulp of his Naked and Famous. "Before we start drinking for real." Maude, with her glass of Barolo, laughs softly next to him in adoration.

"I overheard some of the owners talking." His eyes draw the table in with each syllable.

"Apparently," Chase continues, swinging his neck in Reese's direction. "In the six months that you've been at Pallet, your error-proof reports are helping to avoid so much overspending, they say our branch is on pace to have yet another record-breaking year in profits."

"Holy shit bruv," Hester says.

"I know, right?!" Chase replies.

"Woah," exclaimed both Luciana and Maude at the same time. They look at each other and start giggling.

"I've seen plenty of people come and go in that office," Hester says, looking into his Vieux Carré.

"Exceeding KPIs like that will get you a promotion, easy-peasy."

Somehow, he's forgotten all about a salesman named Lennie who used to work at Pallet. It's been a few years since he last reached out, but Hester's always too busy to keep in touch.

"To Reese!" The men's partners cheer, their glasses rising toward the ceiling.

"Yeah!" Hester and Chase chime in. "To Reese!"

"Aw, thanks," Reese says, making the statue want to laugh out loud. The young man thinks he's playing modest, but this is the kind of validation he leaves the house for. The statue notes while Reese loves the attention, it's also making his knee twitch under the table without him realizing.

As the two couples keep discussing their travel plans for 2020, Reese looks to the restaurant's grand ceiling, missing Luciana's comments about reports of some weird flu going around, Maude asking if it could spread into a pandemic, and her husband saying there's no fucking way.

Instead, he's immediately drawn to the small yet intricate cream-colored marble patterns carved or painted like the ceiling of the Sistine Chapel. Casey would probably say it was a Venetian- or Sicilian-inspired mosaic, but all Reese sees is a fancy kaleidoscope. The patterns interlock and flow into colorful grape vines, fig leaves, and papyrus scrolls.

For the second Reese looks up to gather himself as his friends enjoy anecdotes, jokes, and asides, he tries to follow the circular yet flowing motif that radiates across the entire ceiling. But his eyes are trapped, following endless loops as the patterns start to move and change color, some emerging in 3D.

Reese has no idea where anything starts and ends at this point. Then he locks eyes with the big-titty, immensely engorged statue. He could swear it just winked at him. The statue looks like it's about to mouth something to Reese before a familiar voice breaks him from the trance.

"Whatcha looking at?" a woman asks as she approaches the table. A warm hand comes to rest on Reese's shoulder as the other reaches for the watering Last Word.

"You must be Casey!" the two couples at the table say with inclusive joy, their second drink kicking in.

Reese glances behind himself at Casey. She's taking off her black-and-grey peacoat, revealing a long-sleeved turtleneck and red skirt.

Even the statue is enthralled with her Black Irish—almost blue—hair, milky-white skin, and dark-brown eyes. As is everyone else at the table, except Reese.

The statue looks solemnly at Reese as he only recalls her having a particularly gnarly bowel movement this morning.

"Hi, everyone!" Casey says with a quick gasp to catch her breath from rushing in and fighting the February cold.

At least spring was coming soon, and the world was open to endless possibilities and even greater times.

"Sorry I'm late!"

"No problem!" Hester says. Reese hears a cough from somewhere above, looking around for a second, before suddenly remembering to properly introduce Casey to everyone.

He goes around the table and tells Casey what everyone at the table does: Luciana being a teacher and Maude a civil engineer. As Luciana reaches for her glass of Amarone della Valpolicella, her three-carat ruby ring gives off a gleam of passion in the low light.

"Oh. My. God," Casey says, noticing the woman's jewelry. "That ring is GORGEOUS!"

The statue agrees.

"Oh. My. God," Reese thinks to himself. The statue can only wonder why he already wants to change the subject.

"Why, thank you!" Luciana says, playfully twinkling her fingers in an attempt to recreate the refraction.

"That reminds me," Casey says. The statue watches Reese's mouth open ever so slightly, nearly without thought.

"Please don't," Reese tries to casually whisper in Casey's ear.

"I have a question for you all," she says in an earnest bid for connection with her man's friends. "You know, since we're all couples here."

"Ooooh," Maude says

"What?" Chase asks.

"I'll allow it," Hester says, clearly joking.

"Go for it!" Luciana beckons her, clearly interested.

"She asks this every time we're around couples," Reese groans to himself softly.

"How did everyone meet?" Casey asks with bottomless curiosity.

There's a deafening silence that seems to last as long as the drive on your first date. Everyone looks at Casey, then Reese, then to their respective partners, before bursting into laughter.

"That's a great question," Hester says.

"It's actually a really funny story," Luciana adds.

"I was dating Luciana's roommate at the time," Hester says, starting their story.

"But she always went to bed super early and hated going out on the town. So I would just hang out with her roommate, who was cool."

Luciana tries to hide her blush with her hand as Hester recalls their budding attraction to one another.

"Then we all went on this group trip to Thailand for spring break, and Luciana and I kissed under the moon one night while everyone was asleep," he says.

"It must have been a week, tops, before they broke up and Hester started coming by the apartment—to see me," Luciana says in a proud display of her worth.

Reese reminds himself to keep his jaw off the fancy white tablecloth as the statue glows at the story. Reese looks around to make sure what he just heard was correct; because everyone at the table is wide-eyed and riveted by the torrid affair-turned-love.

"What happened to the roommate?" asks Chase.

"Oh, she subleased her room and transferred to a university in the Netherlands the next semester." Luciana says. "She doesn't reach out when she visits. I wonder why."

"Right?" Hester says. "Us three used to have so much fun together."

"She's probably just busy with her life," says Chase. "That's exactly how it was before Maude and I got together."

"Oh??" Hester, Luciana, and Casey say at the same time, heads nodding attentively in the same direction.

"Yeah. I was out in Vegas, scribing contracts for chips and fuckin' living it," Chase says. "But then I got a call that my little brother died, so I flew back to the County for the funeral and to help his young family for a few weeks."

"And he never left!" Maude says, giggling.

There's something going around with Tom Delonge from Blink-182 shaking his head in confusion, saying, "What the fuck..." That meme is seared into Reese's mind as Chase and Maude explain the phenomenon of grief causing wacky things, with everything happening for a reason.

Reese remembers how Maude visits the office with their kids all the time. But their older kids are in high school, while they welcomed twins last year.

The statue chuckles, watching Reese do the math and wonder if the kids call each other siblings or cousins.

Seconds later, a rumble in his pocket snaps Reese from his disbelief. Subtly, he reads a new text from Rebecca under the table. The statue playfully wonders why the man's body is ever so slightly shifted from his girlfriend.

Rebecca: How's dinner? Wanna puke yet?

Reese tries to fire off a quick reply before Hester speaks up.

"What about you two, Reese and Casey?" he asks.

Reese looks back up to the ceiling, to the statue, and starts to answer. But perhaps it's the gin in his drink. Or maybe the dinner table slid into such an honest space that his words came forth without thought.

"Oh, we met on my first day at Pallet."

He looks back at the table, expecting the ooh's and ahh's of a sappy love story. Instead, he finds Chase,

Hester, Maude, Luciana, and even Casey with their heads tilted in confusion.

"We met in grad school?" Casey says, half-questioning reality. "Are you alright?" she asks with concern, noticing his phone light up in his lap.

He's about to answer when his phone buzzes again. The two couples at the table look at each other and watch in awkward silence.

"And who's Rebecca?" Casey asks her boyfriend.

"Oh, shit!" Chase blurts out, his wife elbowing him in the ribs.

The servers have yet to take the table's entree orders. Meanwhile, the statue gazes at Pallet's data analyst. The words don't know how to come out of Reese's mouth as he looks back to the ceiling for another brief yet endless second.

Yet somehow, it seems like the forever of a wedding vow and the draining end of a divorce, only lasting a second as Reese tries to make a sound.

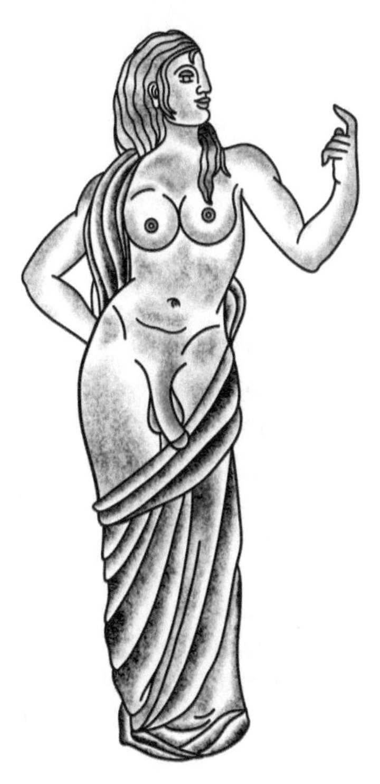

Wobblestrut

I shuffle my way past Old Man Weston's bungalow, not far from the Avenue, when I hear him go:

"Well, hot dog, Wobblestrut," he says. "I need your help again, boy!"

"Whatchu want, whatchu need?" I say, walking up to the man's rickety porch, the summer sun setting on my neck.

"I know you're drunk on your way to some more," Weston says. Bleach-white hamburger meat pops out from his white wifebeater; though I know if there's any beating going on, it's his ol' lady who's liable to use her fingers.

"But Sherrl heard something in the basement—it might stew well," Weston adds, rubbing his pot belly and exhibiting a linty belly button for the street to see.

"Why don't ya get it for us, and we'll put something in ya belly before you run the tavern dry?" he says, trying to sweeten the deal.

"Shew! Before they run me dry!" I say right on back, as he don't gotta ask me twice after saying all that. I rub the ingrown hair on my Adam's apple, and now that I think about it, I ain't had a damned thing since this morning with my rum and pickled herring.

A pale figure appears from behind Weston, checking to see who he's talking to. It's his wifey, Sherrl. A porcelain of a woman also in her sixties, I'd say she weighs about one-forty and is three whole feet taller than me—maybe two more than her hubby.

Understanding my current predicament, I look at the old man with the funny new posture, leaning on one leg, rosy-cheeked wife at his side, and give them a counteroffer they can't refuse.

"Boil me an egg and gimme something strong to sip as an appetizer, too," I say as I wipe the sweat off my patched scalp with my dirt-browned pocket tee that's starting to match my leathering skin.

Showcasing the good snaggle on the right side of my smile with the gold cap, I saunter up to their door and enter on into their little abode.

As Momma would say, the interior of their little rancher is something out of a movie. On the walls in the living room above old, shaggy, velvet-green couches are groundhog heads hung like prized game from the Sahara.

Weston likes to shoot em' with his namesake because they won't stop eating his tomatoes—he thinks.

I'm lucky the ol' bastard hasn't put a ball of lead

in my behind, as I be the one stealing them tasteless tomatoes. See, he's too boring to know what they taste like at 3 a.m. when the bar kicks ya out on your ass.

But then again, me and ol Wessie go way back. I've had so many jobs in my fifty-sumn years, and nearly all of em' came through Weston.

Sherrl hands me a peeled hard-boiled egg and a tin cup of homebrew as I take a seat on the couch, with Weston snug in the recliner in front of the tube. I retrieve a can of Old Bay from my sock for both the egg and the drink as Weston grunts a burp, jamming his panhandle-tanned thumbs on the remote control to the disco music video channel.

This is life around here in Buss Ask, Maryland, even though people get the name misconstrued as Buss 'Ass' all the time.

Basically, Buss Ask is like two halves to one beer bottle cap. You got the side on the top with the logo— that's the yuppy part of town with all the remodeled homes. Where the momos in suits take bougie lunches and go to foo foo happy hours. Them never get the 'Ask' wrong when referring to their side, their boroughs. But I know they, and them County folk, homage our bottom side of the cap with 'Ass.'

I be around. And it's often the same people talking who don't admit popping in, when nobody's looking, to get their fill of our shine, pine, and sublime—if ya feel me.

But I digress. Here in Buss Ass, we gots cable tv with the color and take care of each other real nice. People think this part is just dumps, but it's more than that. Hell, one time ol' Wessie hid me from the law after I took their horse for a ride off the shine!

But now since his surgery, he don't do too much other than sit in his chair. The doctors said he'll get full mobility after the procedure, but it's been some time since Ol' Wessie can't do too much but enjoy a disabled retirement.

Luckily, he gots Wobble the hottie handyman—with the resilience of a sewer rat—to once again save the day!

I finish the egg and down the swill as I look on in horrified amusement at Weston dancing in the recliner. It's to some music video talking about a radio star playing on the tv, and here this boy is spinning his hips around in moon circles. Sherrl luckily retrieves me a few moments later to show me the mouth of a narrow flight of stairs leading down the basement. Looking into the deep dark in front of me, she gives me a candle with a tiny bead of flame.

"Let me know when ya get it, hun," she says softly as she walks away into the kitchen. "I'm already peeling the onions."

Descending down the stairs into the dank basement, the little drop of flame from Sherrl's candle is the only light leading me to where I'm going.

Hell, if it weren't for light and vision in general, I probably wouldn't be called Peabody Wobblestrut—the royal drunk who makes a stupor look like a conqueror's procession on golden pavement. They'd probably just call me Drunk Accident who pees on hisself.

I manage to get halfway down the stairs when I

think to myself about that one time I was boosting copper wire and saw Old Weston arguing with some of the boys at the hardware store about rancher homes not having basements. They called him an idiot and shew! That boy whooped all three before I heard them finish the word 'idiot.'

But after the surgery, Wessie can't do none of that now. Which again, is why my sober self is handling his domestics.

Ew, sober. But then, like I imagine Einstein was thinking, I remember the scientific opportunity directly in front of me. The literal flame making my way.

I figure it's time for a little chemical fusion. Fumbling in the chest pocket of my shirt, I keep trekking down the stairs as I retrieve my modified cigarette. Ingeniously emptied and repacked with something wacky; plus a little embalming fluid and cardamom. Using the flame for a lighter, I light my roll, letting myself take a few more drags to keep this life—I mean day—going.

The buss down, if you will. Maybe that's where the 'Buss' around here comes from.

This would've come in perfect after I got thrown out the bar this morning. But I couldn't find my matches. I bet Rithie has 'em, that 600-pound bum with the neckbeard. I woulda beat the ugly off him years ago if he hadn't stopped me from walking into a mine all them years ago in the jungle.

I inhale the remaining wisps of smoke from the pits of my lungs, blowing out the mixed tobacco, feeling wackier as I finish my flight down the stairs, feeling almost like I'm walking up.

Reaching the bottom of the stairs, I sit the candle on the banister and look around.

"Alright, where's dinner?" I say out loud.

All I can barely see in the dark is an unfinished, dank basement with a bunch of boxes, old furniture, and a bookshelf. There're also mannequins on mannequins lined up like the Terracotta Army in one corner. Except they're not in armor or holding any weapons.

They're decked out to the finest in different pieces of flair from the past; clad in intricately patterned shirts and slacks, leather chaps, gator slippers, and extravagant wigs. From Soul Train afros to Farrah Faucett feathers and ones with dreadlocks. Wigs of all kinds were down here.

I yell up and ask who in the hell these belong to—Weston says they're his. I have heard ol' boy had a colorful time in the eighties.

I grin as he says I can wear one of the blonde wigs.

Using the old rubber band I found on the ground, I put on the wig with long, blonde hair, fixing it with my first ponytail ever. Peekin' at the old wardrobe mirror by the wall, something takes over me—like I've been meaning to say it my entire life—as I speak to myself.

"Wobble?!" I say.

"Mhmh??" I say back.

"Hot damn, you looking mint, boy!"

I mean, if I'm gonna be honest, I've always wanted a ponytail—but can only grow a rat's.

But now that I'm dashingly equipped, I'm gonna

mess around and pull it off better than that Matthew McConaughey fella. I smile at the immaculate reflection that is I, wiping the blonde bangs out my eyes.

Then, just as suddenly, I hear a faint rattle coming from somewhere here in the basement. It's not easy for me to stand still, and I always got something ringing in my ear. But I'll find whateva's down here if I stay quiet.

Using the cracked leather couch as support like I'm pretending to be blind for dollars, I close my eyes to listen for the critter, betting it's a mouse. Or maybe even a raccoon, if we're lucky.

But it's then that my head feels a lil funny; like I'm falling inside of some sort of whirling tunnel vision. Kinda like when Rithie and I first tried absinthe, and all we did was meow at each other all night.

When I open my lids, I'm surrounded by small houses in a wide backyard. Somehow, I'm back home; real home, where Momma has eggs and grits on the stove first thing in the morning. The home that's now a shopping center, with Momma six feet to kingdom come. Years before I ever became Peabody Wobblestrut.

I still have my ponytail, though, hot dog!

I look around and can see Momma's floral apron and the back of her poodle clip from our window, already whipping up my favorite: spare ribs and mashed potatoes with the goat cheese, shew!

I'm sitting on a plastic four-wheeler by the creek next to the house, rippin' and roarin' with my buddy, Noz. Oh, we'd race down this little grass hill and stop our brakes right before we ran into the creek and caught minnows! I remember how this day went all those years ago, riding down that damned hill and peddling my little wobbles at full speed to drag the brake at the bottom. Just like the heroes in the movies do.

Without realizing it, I'm zooming down the hill, dragging my brake impeccably. Nozzie said I was so cool; I always thought he was, too.

I'm waiting at the bottom by the creek when he goes, and dammit he's peddling way faster than I, gaining way more speed than me! His drag is going to be so cool I remember thinking. Then and now, that boy coulda been the next action man on television. But right when it's time to stop dramatically and show the bad guys what's up, his pedal locks.

He's going way too fast.

"No—" I barely manage before my first friend speeds right on through and falls into that damn creek.

The last time this happened, my legs couldn't work for some reason, and I had to watch him sink into the creek. I tried to scream out for Momma, for Supaman, someone, but my audio stayed muted; no matter how hard I tried to yell. He didn't even really make a sound the whole time either, just his beige arms doing a lot of flailing, then none. The messy brown shag of a mop on his head bobbed up and down a lot, then just stayed down.

I never saw Noz again, and it took his family weeks to find him.

"But not this time, I declare!" I say as my hot Wobblestrut self jumps right off my wheelie, gets them bangs out my face, and dives right into that creek.

I'm like one of them manatees you see at Sea World, wading in that blue, unforgiving water as I rescue my pal this time around. I scoop that boy up and do one of them backstroke things with my legs 'til we get back on land.

I get us both out the water as we take large gasps for air, larger than after the harshest bong rip of your life. All these years passed and I could barely remember what ol' Nozzie-Boy looked like. But looking at him in this moment, I see him getting his breath together and making sounds. It's like his missing two front teeth and hazel eyes never vanished from my memory and were always seared into my brain.

"Thanks, Moses," Noz says with another gasp of air as I hug my best buddy before we both get distracted by the sound of something shuffling around.

We look at each other in confusion, trying to discern where it's coming from, and the next thing I know, I'm no longer at the creek. Instead, I'm once again falling into a spiral of nothingness.

Out of nowhere, I'm in my very best, years later, inside the church down the street. Nowadays, I've been known to drain the snake or purge some poison behind the joint. But this time, Nozzie-Boy's right next to me instead of Rithie. The sun's brighter than at the creek, and there's my Momma and Pawpaw sitting in the front row.

It takes me a moment, but it all comes to me, I remember what's going on and why the place is, was, packed.

Everyone's here to see me on my big day with the love of my life, Adaline May.

They all used to say how beautiful her almond skin, wavy peach hair, and dark-brown eyes looked with the white dress that rested gracefully down her upper shins. And how her love for me was painted all over her freckles, like one of them laser beams illuminating the halls; walking down the aisle with her goateed goblin of a father.

But I see it all this time, very clearly. Maybe it's because my belly's not swishing like a washing machine from the jug of moonshine me and Rithie chugged right before the ceremony last time.

I don't even remember the pastor being this warm and articulate as she ordains our union in front of loved ones and God, but shew! She coulda had her own radio show!

Adaline exchanges her vows first, as she's always desired since she was a little girl. She tells me how much she loves me, how she fell in love with me the minute she saw me get off the ship from redeployment.

I'm tearing up so much right now, I can't even see her long, curls poking from under her hairdo and veil. Like a goddess trying to spare me, a mere mortal, from her numinosity.

Then the pastor asks ol' me to go. But lemme say something: this time will be different!

I won't get a shine burp and toss my cookie contents all over my bride-to-be in front of the entire congregation. Man, I remember how quick Rithie and I hightailed it out of here the last time, and I never saw my Adaline May again.

I hear she's Adaline Ricci now, with one of them boys she had with the doctor with the mole on his neck running for senator. The other thinks he's something because he runs some fancy I-talian joint out in the County.

And when I say I laid my vows down this time y'all, I sure did, boy! I tell her everything I've said to myself since—cold, drunk, and sore—for all them years. How I wish I was still her Moses Patrick. And how she'll love me so much more now that I got myself a ponytail! I can't kiss her quicker this time, y'all, when the pastor said we was mister and missus Cornett.

But the instant I feel them luscious lips touch mine, I don't feel the luxurious blessing of love

Instead, we look at each other, lip-locked and confused, as we hear something pattering, and I find myself falling right back in that familiar blur.

And before I know it, my beautiful Adaline May is no longer in front of me. Nor is my best buddy Noz beside me.

Instead, I'm back in Weston's funky-ass basement!

I'm not fussing, though; ain't no such thing as a bad trip, I always say. Noz was a real sharp best man this time around, and I bet ol' boy met hisself a bridesmaid—or three—that night, I think to myself as I grin at the mirror.

And Adaline, my what a bride. I'll always love that woman, and I'm sure we woulda named at least one of ours after her Grammy.

There ain't much to talk about past that, as the sounds of something moving behind the bookcase snap me fully to the present. I walk toward the bookshelf and push it gently aside a few inches to investigate.

Lowering the candle to the ground, I can't believe my glazed-over, watery eyes as I'm met with a tiny lizard. I mean salamander. One of those red-backed ones with the line down their backs, right here in front of Peabody Wobblestrut in a stylish ponytail! But this one is bright red all over; one of them mutants.

"Erythristic," I say with a soft whistle.

Now, I may imbibe, but I know my amphibians. And this ain't fit for no soup. This here's a royal weirdo, just like me. We lock eyes, and I swear I heard it call out to my suave self.

"Say, fool, getmeoutthisgoddamnedbasement!"

So naturally, I put the critter in my shirt pocket, move the shelf back, get my candle, and make my way to the stairs, eventually ascending the narrow flight—even though I'm regrettably kinda coming down.

Sherrl and Weston are still watching music videos on the couch in the living room when I return from the basement and tell them I couldn't find nothing, demanding an onion for all my troubles.

After offering to teach them how to dance, I run out the house; saying I was keeping the ponytail.

Sherrl just asks "Why?", but Weston yells, "NO!"

Ogre on the Avenue

R ed and blue lights blare off the silver badge of a
fortyish-year-old white man in a dark, navy-blue
jacket as he gets out of his squad car and into hysteria
on the busiest block in Buss Ass, Maryland.

It's zero three hundred, and the street is flooded with
more squad cars, fire trucks, and one lone ambulance.
The officer looks around the scene as he shakes one of
his direct reports from dazing at the ground.

"Calm down, rook. What's going on?" says the man.

The thousands of habitués swarming the first
responders are a bunch of, in the older cop's mind,
dumb kids in their twenties drinking and smoking
themselves silly. In fact, not far in age from the rookie
in front of him.

"It's Sugar Al," the young officer manages to
report to his captain. The young man, light-toned
but racially ambiguous, has been on the force for a
few years, seen it all, yet is still considered a shoat

by the veteran barrows. In the dead of Summer 2023, without a drop of rain in sight, the man's uniform is somehow an even darker blue, damp with sweat, fear, and utter confusion.

"Don't fuck with me." says the captain. "Who the hell is ballsy or dumb enough to shoot the king of 900 Avenue?"

"Cap, he wasn't shot," the young officer replies, trying to keep his wits from what he responded to just minutes before, then adding:

"And whatever got him, I don't think a man has anything to do with it."

I remember my last day as king very well; as any good pimp should.

Put it this way: If you live every day like it's your last and savor each fleeting moment like the blessings they are, then you, too, will have no issue looking back—when it's your turn.

Take notes, pimpin'. This is your first playa tip from ya boy, Sugar Al.

But I suppose it would make better sense to mention what I remember dreaming about before my day even started.

I was inside a tiny sub and wing joint, the type we get after bar hopping and watching booties twerk. Except it wasn't 3 a.m., with no bro or broad in sight.

The streets beyond the glass windows of this tiny spot were completely empty. Not a single car, not even a streetlight was on.

I took a seat at the only table with a light on hanging from above, as if I already knew why I was here. Feeling like forever and a millisecond at the same time, I was met on the other end of the table with a cow, pig, and lamb. With a matter-of-fact moo, snort, and bleat, they together said something I understood and accepted—mammals to mammal.

"Marked."

The word hung like a verdict as I felt a pinch on my ankle and shook my leg feverishly. A tiny bug that didn't look like a spider, with eight legs and a white star on its back, scurried from the end of my pressed slacks. Locking eyes with me, it chuckled before skittering off.

My eyes shot open as I woke up to bright natural light at the ass-crack of three in the afternoon in my California King—to the sight of ass-cracks draped in deep-red satin sheets. They, the cheeks, belonged to a many of goddesses, several women sprawled in leisurely slumber and arranged in an edible arrangement of skin tones, styles, and homelands.

I remember Emiko was there, my fair-skinned piece from the East, draped in a pink kimono. Next to her laid Brittiny, my kinky Canadian, wearing nothing but a blue tuque.

And of course there was Shantel—my number one girl, my alleluia from Nubia—snuggled under my arm, home-grown braids down to her dimples of Venus. She say she love me, I always told her she should.

There were a few more nymphs in the mix as well. None of them ever left my high-rise on the nice side of town after meeting me, just once, and having the time of their lives. You'd be surprised how impressed ladies get when they can retrieve ice from your fridge's door; not from a funky ice tray you gotta manually refill like a slave.

I tightened the burgundy satin robe that matched the sheets, real playa shit, and went immediately to the restroom.

If there's one thing a good pimp does, it's to always stay fresh. People say some silly shit about their first cup of coffee, or whatever. I don't even know who the fuck you are until I've flossed, banged on some mouth wash in the shower, and then brushed my teeth when I'm done. Which was exactly what I did after waking up.

Playa tip: Don't even ask if I did anything else in there bodily. Like ladies, playas gotta keep things to themselves, too.

Also, I don't fuck with that Dove or Axe shit, who do you think I am? I know an Arabian spot in the city that makes a superb bar soap with turmeric, and shit. It lathered this immaculate vessel and the aggry beads around its neck well. After getting a good suds going, I used my African net and exfoliated my body. It's like honey for the birds and bug repellant for broke niggas.

Don't forget to get your lips, too; they'll look smooth and juicer for ladies who wanna kiss you, ya dig?

Reaching down my legs, I ran the net gently over a sore on my ankle. I probably got it while taking a bunny named Becca for a stroll in the park last week. Either way, it's taking its sweet time healing. Sugar Al doesn't wait for anything, and it better not leave a scar.

Looking in the mirror before I reacquaint myself as a humble host to my goddess guests of maiden honor, I couldn't help but look at the man, the myth, the fresh-to-death Alphonze Galley looking right back at him. Black and proud, with wavy, permed black hair with enough oil and grease to rival the Permian, I matched my signature style with a finely lined up faint mustache with black diamond studs in both ears.

"Hurry, Al, we're getting cold!" I heard Shantel, Emiko, and Britt call from the bed behind the all-white bathroom wall, giggling like they started a tickle fight.

I ignored them and opened the mirror's cabinet, grabbed my matching diamond fronts, and fitted them on the bottom row of my teeth. Afterwards, I reached for a hydrocolloid patch and slapped it on my ankle.

Closing the cabinet and looking at myself with a grin I couldn't hide for the death of me, I expected this to be an ordinary Tuesday.

Later on, after I showed my guests some yoga maneuvers and toys they've never seen before, I dressed myself in brown pressed slacks, a free-flowing black silk shirt, and gator loafers to match. I went with a diamond bracelet to go with my grill and earrings on this fateful day.

I don't live with many regrets in life, but one is that I can't remember what the women wore. I do remember thinking they all looked bad as fuck.

We left the penthouse around ten and hopped in Juice, my orange H2 Hummer. I was driving the boat, Shantel's riding passenger, with the rest of the women packed in the back like sardines. It only takes bout five minutes before Juice strode through Buss Ask into the shitty part that everyone calls 'Ass.' I fondly remember having one hand gripped firmly on the wheel the entire ride, the other playing with Shantel's g-string.

Passing a few sex shops along the way, Emiko asked what the plans were on the Avenue tonight. But before I give my answer, her ass can wait—and let me explain 900 Avenue. The most poppin' block in Buss Ass.

During the day, everyday people get their groceries, dry cleaning, and haircuts and take their kids for ice cream. And there's plenty of boutiques, plant stands, and pop-up stands open as long as the sun's out. Outside of real-life amenities like schools, hospitals, and that type of shit, the 900 has everything you need.

Especially once that sun sets, giving families and decent folk a few hours to vacate. Because by nightfall, 900 Avenue was a completely different monster.

All the safe for work establishments and boutiques shuttered, as if the Avenue's legion of dive bars, dance halls, and lifestyle clubs just finished their breakfast. Bright neon lights from these nocturnal establishments of carousing strobed the Avenue as young adults, in body or in spirit, packed the sidewalks and partied into dawn.

And when that time came, sadly enough, so came a quiet hour of rest before the Avenue's cafés and grocery stores brought their early morning crews, signaling another day in the city on a street.

Before we got there, around 10:30, I parked Juice along the side of a road, as even goddesses get hungry—remember that. And in my case, Britt had the great idea of getting hot dogs from a dusty cart with an even dustier dude peddling them. Niggas like these always have some sort of sob story, and this one said he's raising money for some sort of lizard exhibit.

He looked like Buss Ass incarnate, the shittiest, with patched up clothes and a cheap gold cap. To be honest, blud, I wasn't tryna eat from a drunk. But I can't blame these fine dimes for chasing adventure, even in their goofy food choices. I remember looking at them, thinking this on some empathy-type shit.

Still, I obliged and got a few franks for myself since I had to admit, I was getting hungry myself.

Plus, his blonde ponytail was cold as fuck.

Woofing down my third dog, it was barely eleven, and people were already packing the sidewalks as Juice strolled down the Avenue. Getting lucky and running three green lights in a row, we pulled up to the hottest club on the Avenue.

The Lily Pad—my spot.

Nobody's crowds are as hot as the Pad's. The top gentlemen's club in Buss Ass, I've shared drinks and seen some of the biggest wigs in Bussy too many times to count. Professors, janitors, mailmen, politicians, cops—you fuckin' name it. It's why they call me the king around here!

I parked Juice right in front of the Pad, cars having to make room around me to pass. I took a quick rub at my ankle as one of my valets, fresh out of community college, immediately greeted us before taking my keys.

"Good evening, Mr. Sugar." He bowed and turned to my entourage of goddesses. "L-Ladies."

He bowed again, now to them, in part to hide his growing blush and fear of looking at their chests. I chuckled softly, watching the young man, who reminded me of my younger self, as I tipped him a Lincoln and headed inside.

Crowded lines of people were still wanting to get in as my security guards in black-tie suits, biceps nearly ripping their shirts, greeting us at the door.

If you ever hire security, make sure you don't just pick the biggest and blackest nigga. He gotta be bald too, and make sure he has at least three hot dogs rolled in the back of his head.

"Evening, boss," one of the guys said. "What do you want me to do with this one?"

I looked to my right and saw a fat-ass white dude with a neckbeard arguing with a dusky-toned woman with glasses and a buzzcut. She wore nothing but a thin neon string, showing nothing but skin. I thought I told Rithie's musty ass to not come back until he had money to pay his tab. The last time his nasty ass was here, he came in wearing thin sweatpants and tried paying for a VIP session with pissy Monopoly money.

"I'll take care of him," I remember saying as I walked up to the Buss Asshole. I heard the tail end of him promising to sign over his next winning scratch-off before he saw me get close.

"Oh, hey, Sugar Al," Rithie started to stammer out, "I was just tellin—"

Nigga didn't even get to finish his stupid sentence before I backhanded him with the power of all the pimps and playas before me, sending ripples across his jowl. Hitting my floor with a thunderous thud and tripping the Richter scale, he started groaning on the floor like a beached whale as I looked at both of my guards.

"Send him on his way," was all I said as they each huffed, taking one arm each, and dragging the man's pitiful self out the club.

I pardoned my manners before the woman he'd been bothering and slipped her a few Lincolns as my crew and I hit a flight of stairs subtly in the far back, walking upstairs where nobody's allowed.

When we entered my private office, we're met with the familiar view of tinted windows overlooking the entire club, our reflections mirrored in the ceiling. From this high vantage point, we could see each stage, with each alluring acrobat's athleticism on display.

One dancer was upside down while scaling her pole. Another was moonwalking to Radiohead in 9-inch heels. And towards the back I saw security inflating the pool for sumo wrestling; the Jell-o packet in one guard's hand told me it was a key lime night.

And for hours, we lodged in that office, having the best booth in the house. It was a wonderful montage of drinking and blowing hydro—like we do every night. I smiled as I turned to everybody enjoying themselves and seeing nothing but ass, pleased with what I'd created for myself, running things like some sort of heavenly pirate. I looked up at the mirrored ceiling and remember thinking how we had this same kind of revelry every night, like it was the last night of our lives—if any of us were paying attention.

But by the time my boys came through, I started to feel like shit. I was happy, king of the Avenue, but I could feel my lips a little juicier—and not like how I was saying in the shower. I felt a tightness in my wrist as the diamond-piece started pinching my skin.

At one point, the bald-headed woman from before sat on my lap, thanking me for earlier and asking if I'd like to take a shot with her. I remember thinking she's just my type, but I surprisingly declined, finding it harder to swallow. When the waitress, butterfly tattoo poking out of her booty shorts, swayed by for another round of drinks, I nearly made her trip from surprise when I requested hot tea with honey.

My face started to hurt, and I could feel the faint lines of future wrinkles and creases on my face starting to deepen.

Within an hour, swallowing, breathing, and even talking started to become labor-intensive. It didn't help that everyone around me—my goddesses and homies—started to look at me with sheer horror instead of immediate concern.

My boys tried to stay calm, but they looked like they were seeing a dead man walking. The women started screaming and crying.

"SOMEBODY CALL 911!" Shantel yelled out.

With all the alcohol flowing through me and bodies in proximity, I've never felt cold here at the Pad. But now, I was shaking with violent frigidness. I remember standing up to maybe find a bathroom before thumping unceremoniously to the floor.

Next thing I knew, out of nowhere, came some dirty-ass piglet asking me if I was alright. I couldn't tell if the nigga was Puerto Rican or just light-skinned—but regardless—I didn't wanna say shit to him and woulda spit in his face.

My back to the ground and eyes were barely able to open, I saw the last memory of Sugar Al in the mirrored ceiling. The handsome thing that was he; covered in hives, looking like a thousand bees stung him.

His eyes were essentially swollen shut, and he was unable to speak full sentences. Before everything went silent—I mean dark—the last thing I managed to hear was that bug's chaotic laughter and that bald chick gasping a single word:

"Ogre!"

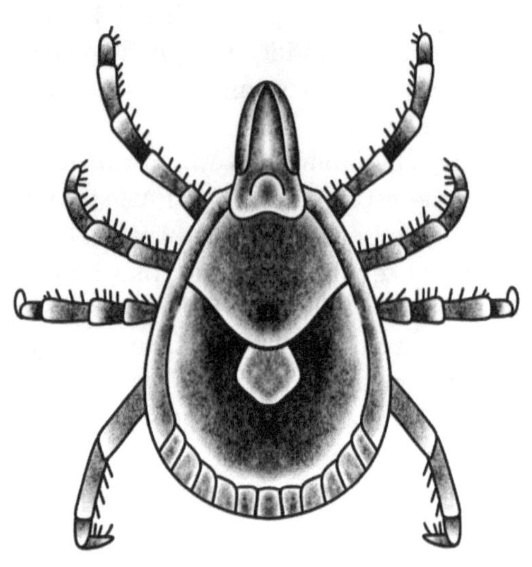

II. Newlife:
Dino, The Scam Sprout

8:25 reads the clock on the dashboard of my Honda '97 Accord on 18 September 2025.

The sun looks orange in this autumn morning sky as I'm driving down a quiet back road surrounded by old trees. Their yellowing leaves are also starting to turn orange. I don't remember it being so nice out when I left my parents' place out in the County half an hour ago. Not that I can stop to appreciate the views anyway.

I'm on the way to my new job as an operational specialist at some random farm in a town that my parents call Buss Ass. It's really Buss Ask, but apparently this side of town isn't necessarily the safest in Maryland. They try hiding their feelings and tell me instead how this place is hived with thugs who don't give a fuck and pungent vagrants.

But shit, these guys are paying thirty-five bucks an hour. And for a nobody like me at 25-years-lost, this is the highest wage I've ever stood to earn. Hell, in college I made thirteen dollars an hour tutoring ceramics. And when I got back home and started temping, I was pushing fifteen an hour.

I fucking hate temp agencies.

I mean, the recruiter I worked with last calls me with new assignments all the time. But if I have to sort another warehouse's inventory or catalog thousands of documents stacked in tiny mountains, I just might kill myself by death of a thousand dust mites and papercuts.

I'm serious.

My last assignment was spent preparing fliers for a well-known furniture company around here. But after months of being stuck in a bullpen with entry-levelers who flirted all day, I had to question my career choices.

So I did what any sensible, undergraduated, super-super senior would do. I stopped temping and never looked back as I sought for a real job...

Ending up right on my parents' couch within a year.

I have a Bachelor's degree; it should be easy to find another, better job, I thought.

Yet eight months later, with zero savings, paired with parents who no longer hide their exasperation, the brown eyes that look back at me in the rearview mirror are those of a man with not a single muscle or idea; let alone a clue.

I can't say the same for literally everyone else I'm honored to know. I graduated just like my friends, and they're already making amazing strides as doctors, astronauts, administrators, and shit. I even know people making music and movies.

Yet everywhere I go, here I am: Dino Toilston,

driving up to an obscure farm nobody's heard of, hoping it's not a scam. I mean, everything about this job is just too good to be true. Their health benefits are incredible, with eighty percent of my premium covered, a ten-dollar deductible, and a massive provider network.

They'll match seven percent of my simple IRA, while promising annual bonuses—plural? Just to work on a dusty farm Monday through Friday from 9 a.m. to 5 p.m.

Which begs several questions:

What kind of "farm" is this? The fuck they grow; Opium? Weed?

Do they grow anything?

"What if I'm what they aim to farm?" I say to myself.

I was anemic as a kid once; my organs must be worthless. Shit, one of my cousins has sickle-cell.

"This has to be some fucking scam," I say out loud as I veer off the road onto a gravel driveway with a small wooden sign with "Found Farms" carved into it.

8:28 reads my car clock as I pull into a clearing and put my busted Accord in park. Looking around from my driver's side window, I see maple trees, oaks, bushes, and a flower bed surrounding a small rectangular office covered in English ivy. Lining it are knockout roses in a rainbow of colors, hydrangeas that remind me of cotton candy, and too many ferns to count.

Don't ask how I know so much about them; I've read so much Victorian literature these past eight months that I know, against my will, how fascinated the Brits were with ferns in the 1800s.

But I don't see anything you could say is a farm, per se. What I expected to be a large homestead and stables looks more like one of those temporary offices that developers set up at new construction sites, situated in front of a large privacy fence that hides whatever is behind it. The office kinda reminds me of a shipping container.

Welp, looks like this is a scam after all.

Against my better judgment (maybe it's the ferns), I get out of the car I've had since high school and click the beeper twice to hear an old, croaking beep beep. Before walking into what I preemptively consider my next professional disappointment; I study myself in the car window's reflection to make sure I'm at least presentable.

With skin of fine ebony wood that I got from my father, and the long lashes of my mother, I'm dressed how the owner told me to dress: wear what I'm most comfortable in. I chose some stonewashed jeans; checkered Vans; grey, long-sleeved henley; and a green snapback with a slightly curved bill.

I don't even reach the front steps before an olive-toned woman in her late thirties with bobbed black hair—wearing a coral crop top, light denim pants, and dark-tan work boots—greets me. She's a lot taller than I imagined her, probably pushing six feet. I remember her warm, popcorn voice from when I interviewed over the phone. Her name's Winifred.

"Hi...Dino? Right on time, I see!" she chirps as she swings the door open. Jovial for so early in the day.

"Good morning, Winifred." I say with a professional smile and tone I find fake. "Yes, I'm very excited to start."

"Oh, just call me Freddie!" She chuckles. "Let's go inside and get all the housekeeping out of the way before Mr. Apollo gets in. I know he's excited for you to start today."

She crooks her neck for a moment so she can meet my eyes. A tinge of anxiety creeps up my spine as I nod and follow her up the stairs and into the office. But right as I pass her through the open door, she adds.

"He wants to have a one-on-one with you when he arrives."

"G-great!" I manage to spurt out.

I'm going to be fucking sick. It's usually after one of those one-on-ones that both the employer and I realize this won't be a good fit.

I sit at an open table and begin filling out employment paperwork. Luckily, the forms don't take long. You know, the typical shit that takes what seems like a mandatory hour of reading and signing away my rights and first-born child, sheet after sheet. But while I'm wrapping it up, Freddie brings me a cup of straight black coffee—ew—and starts to talk about the office as she takes a seat in a chair by the door.

"Did you notice that we're inside an old shipping container right now?" she asks between sips of coffee, her eyes widening as she emphasizes the interior.

She didn't have to say it like that. Regardless, I may have been distracted from taking my own sip and trying not to recoil, but looking around, I realize I really am inside a shipping container! The walls are insulated, drywalled, and painted an eggshell white that soaks in the natural light from the two windows facing the front of the property.

Not only do I see an air conditioning unit, but everything else you'd want in an office. There's a tiny kitchen, a bathroom, desk space, and even a little futon I can imagine napping on. The space has good taste, too, with artwork strung all over the walls. My favorite is a photo by Ansel Adams that hangs right by the door.

Shiiit, this wouldn't make for a bad apartment.

But still, it's obvious what the bones of this office are, as Winifred points to a side wall that looks like the unmistakable metal door of a shipping unit. Must have been the original door for the container.

"In fact, Mr. Apollo outfitted this office himself with help from friends," she says with a finger pointing upwards, rising from her seat to briefly check the thermostat. Then she adds with a wink, "We even have solar panels on the roof, so there's no power bill!"

I've never heard of this, someone turning a storage unit into a business space. Not to mention using renewable energy, too.

"Half the time, he's not even here." She pouts playfully. "After getting this place sorted"—she looks around, laughing—"the man couldn't help but do it all over again somewhere else!"

"He was just checking on his akiya getaway near Shibuya," she adds, "and will be in Lazio in a few weeks to close on a family farmhouse to fit a village!"

This Apollo guy sounds like a pretty smart dude— or rich, I think to myself. Especially since someone as bubbly as Freddie seems to hold him in high regard. I mean, I'm a little impressed, and I haven't even met him yet.

The scam meter's going down a little, but I'm still nervous. All the big personality bosses I've ever met end up assholes.

As Freddie and I chat a little longer, she tells me how she's worked here for almost five years. She used to be in social work but was often overworked and underpaid, so she bartended on the side to get by.

There was a particularly bad Thanksgiving Eve one year when she couldn't help a family in need and then was slammed with overtly forward drunkards visiting their hometown. That's the night she finally talked to a longtime regular perched like an owl at the end of the bar.

By closing time, she not only knew his name, Len Apollo, but he even offered her a job where she could make a real difference and some real fucking money.

Freddie's in the middle of glowing, talking about her own first day here at the farm and what to expect from mine. She's in the middle of saying something about lunch when I hear the unmistakable sound of a car pulling up and someone getting out of it. The car's music blares for a few seconds before the battery cuts off, but I make out the last few lyrics.

An old track from Incubus, perhaps?

I can't see what kind of car it is, or who's coming out of it. But from one of the office windows, I do see one large plume of smoke or vape rise to the sky and lazily dissipate.

"Oop, that must be him!" Freddie chimes with a smile, looking at her phone, which I see reads 9:44.

Seconds later, the office door flings open, and who I can only assume is the boss steps in. The first thing he does is stretch his arms as wide as he can with a huge smile to match, like he's some prodigal son returning to his homeland.

The man couldn't be much shorter than me at five feet eight, but he's an objectively handsome man of color like me, his skin tone more jarrah than ebony. He's dressed in tan linen pants and a cotton button-up covered in frogs, with the first three buttons undone.

A thick, gold Cuban Linx chain sways around his neck, draped and buried in the graying ground beef on his chest, with a matching bracelet on one vascular wrist. On the other, an Armani watch reads what I imagine to be around 9:46.

To top it all off, this middle-aged man is rocking black crocs and a massive gold ring on his pinky finger, right alongside a modest wedding band on the finger next to it.

This guy's dressed too much like a crook for the scam meter to NOT rise.

He takes the aviator sunglasses off his meticulously close-cut and shaped-up hairline, hooking them on his shirt opening. He then turns to Freddie with a good-morning wave and boyish grin that could only be formed from years of colleague familiarity. Immediately after, he pivots his attention to the person next to her—me.

He extends his callused right hand, pinky-ringed and all, with a smile like he's figuring me out.

"You must be Dino," he says with a smirk that reveals a dimple. "I'm Len Apollo. Founder, president, chairman, captain, and CEO of Found Farms."

"N-nice to meet you," I manage to say back while pondering if all those titles are necessary. Both of us can see Freddie slightly shaking her head at the ground from the corner of our eye.

But his handshake is really firm. And the pinky ring is shockingly warm when it makes contact...

"I hear today's your first day as special ops," he says, still shaking my hand.

"I thought it was operational specialist," I smile back, letting my grip naturally dissolve.

"Same thing." He waves with faux nonchalance. "There's a lot we're looking for in that role." He smiles while getting to the point.

"That said, you're with me all today while I give you the full rundown. You cool with that?"

"I'll make sure to pay attention to everything," I reply, telling the truth while thanking my special meter.

Apollo dresses like a sixty-five-year-old Florida retiree, but he couldn't be a day over forty. I continue studying the man. Though he dresses kind of corny, he's still intimidating. Like I'm in front of a brilliant ball of fire.

"Great!" he says. "I'll get my admin crap out the way and then come and get you in about thirty minutes."

He plops into a separate but tiny office in the back corner.

It takes me a bit to remember how to read the hands on the clock hanging on the wall. But it's 10:40 when Apollo returns from the back office and directs me to the metal side door that leads into the property's fenced backyard.

"Ready to see paradise?" he says with another smirk, revealing a sharp dimple. He's trying to get the door open while looking in the opposite direction at me.

"Let's do it," is all I can think to say to keep from smiling and letting his big reveal land. But then a familiar gut starts thinking:

Here's where the scam is revealed. Here's where Freddie clubs me from behind and I wake up stitched together with strangers like a demented bug—or some other fucked-up shit my Gen X parents would say.

I did note that I couldn't see what's back here from the front when I first arrived because of the tall wooden fencing...

Here's where they "farm" us—I mean ME!

Instead, the metal door swings open, and I'm met with an ode to Gaia herself as trees hang succulent fruit, weirdly shaped vegetables grow on plants, and prolific vines trail in every direction.

This farm really isn't a scam. Huh.

The first thing I see are red, green, and yellow apples growing on the same tree. Pumpkins creep all over the ground. Grapes vine over teepee-like trellises.

Tomatoes, peppers, cucumbers, and nearly every other vegetable you can get from a store spread out right here in front of me. Some of them look funny, too; one's like a spikey-looking melon. But before I can get ahead of my eyes, Apollo starts talking, something I suspect he does liberally.

"So, this is Found Farms. I bought this land about ten years ago, and we're now in our fifth year of generating profit."

The scam meter is lowering. This all looks nice so

far, but it could be a front.

"That's why you're here, Dino!" Apollo points to me with a hearty laugh. "I want you to know the inside and out of this farm so that in your role, you can assist Freddie and me in growing the farm even more."

What's up with these people saying "inside"??

I nod in understanding, still looking around and trying to identify the seemingly hundreds of food plants around me as we start touring the property, which I later learn is three-quarters of an acre.

As we peruse rows of fruits, vegetables, and herbs, Apollo explains the farm's composting process and harvesting methods and about each customer I will soon deliver orders to.

Throughout the tour, I see just how diligent Apollo is about this place, despite the fact that it's becoming clear he's a bit stoned. We're near a far corner of the farm, the shipping container barely in sight, when I see trees with big, teardrop leaves and smooth, grey bark. I expect Apollo to say something about the trees, but he completely ignores them and moves on with the tour.

"What about those?" I ask.

"Aw, don't worry about those," he says. "They're not much."

Okay, that was strange. Scam meter's going up.

After a few hours, the tour concludes, and we're back where it began—in front of the office's metal door.

"That's the farm!" Apollo says, seemingly winded from talking nonstop, not to mention belly laughing at his own jokes. "Think you can handle it all?"

"It's a lot to take in," I say as I keep looking over the property. "But I can handle it, no problem."

"Sensational," Apollo says. "Winifred mentioned that, except for liking ferns, you have little to no gardening experience, but I think all that can be learned on the job. Any questions for your bashful boss?"

This nigga is the complete opposite of bashful, but I do have one question. One that I haven't been able to stop thinking about since the second I saw that backyard farm stretching almost an acre, completely hidden in plain sight. I'm too intrigued to not ask this question.

"What started all of this?" I ask.

Apollo looks at me for what seems like forever before bursting out in laughter.

"Great question! Actually, the answer is right to your right," he says.

Before I can fully turn right, Apollo corrects himself with urgency.

"WAIT, left!" he means.

Quickly jerking my head left, I see what I now know as tomato and pepper plants.

"Those are the descendants of what started it all..."

Huh?

"See, Dino," Apollo starts. "Years ago, during a— erm—sabbatical, my wife and I were in a hardware store for a reason I can no longer remember. But I do remember how we walked by those seed stands. At the time, I'd never grown a thing in my life other than my hair, and that woman bet that I couldn't. Can you believe that?"

There's a tone of offense in his voice that I can't tell is joking or not.

"No way," I say.

I see where this is going, I think...

"Sooo," he continues, "I bought some beefsteak tomato seeds and put them in a pot outside. A few days later, they started sprouting, and that hooked me. I ran inside, and luckily, my wife was cooking dinner. I damn near checked her like a lineman as I snatched the jalapeño seeds she was about to throw away right out of her hand and put them into a pot, too."

Interesting.

"I started growing nearly every seed I could get my hands on, and years later, here we are." He sways his arm to emphasize the property.

"What were you doing before all this?" I can't help but ask in response.

"I used to sell shit for yuppies to sit their funky behinds on, then marketed a little sess for a bit."

He glances out over the farm. "Making everybody money but nothing for myself."

"Then how do you pay to keep everything running? Do tomatoes and peppers really sell for that much?" I ask.

Apollo raises an eyebrow at me, seemingly shocked at my inquiry.

"I mean, are you a retired executive?" I stammer out, the words coming from my mouth without my intention. "Or some day trader who's turned a hobby into an enterprise?"

Fuck, I overstepped. This is where the boss usually drops his fun facade and decides this role mysteriously is no longer needed, and I'm sent on my way.

I nearly turn toward the direction of my shitty car, but Apollo opens his mouth.

"Damn, Freddie really picked a clever one," Apollo says with a huff. "I was hoping you'd ask me a question like that."

Huh?

"I'm really excited to have you on board with us. After lunch, you'll get your answer." His tone is uncharacteristically neutral but serious. "In fact, lunch is probably ready now."

He turns toward the smell like a child alert to a pie cooling on the sill.

Wait, I brought my lunch. What kind of place brings lunch for their employees?

Following Apollo and walking right to the center of the farm, I'm met with a paved patio setup with an outdoor kitchen. There's a grill, a fire pit, and picnic tables, but Winifred's stationed at a brick pizza oven.

"You'd be surprised what you can build with the right materials and YouTube," chimes Apollo as he nearly puts his head in the oven to see what's cooking.

"HEY! Get out of there!" says Freddie as she swats her boss away. Then she turns to me. "How was the tour, Dino?"

"It was great. I've already learned a bunch," I reply, still adjusting to all this being an everyday thing around here.

"That's great," she says. "I'd love to hear about it over lunch!"

The lunch Freddie, Apollo, and I have is indescribable. The brick oven pizza is absolutely covered in toppings. We're talking green peppers, onions, mushrooms, pepperoni, fresh garlic, and basil.

"This pizza is amazing," I'm able to say between slices. I'd fully expected to eat chicken Top Ramen and a PB&J, but this is a very welcome surprise.

"Thank you, Dino," Winifred says as she reaches for her second slice. "As you can imagine, everything in it except for the crust and pepperoni was grown right here at Found."

"Dino asked me how Found Farms is funded," Apollo says to Freddie while pointing at me in accusation. "He thought I was some richy playing farmer, can you believe that?"

"No way," Freddie says, playing along and rolling her eyes with a chuckle.

"Right??" Apollo says, with a chuckle. "But anyway, after lunch, I'm taking him to that place."

He smiles mischievously through his eyes.

"I told you he'd be a good fit," she says matter-of-fact, finishing her slice.

"That you did," he says. "Anything you need from me before we head out?" He wipes his mouth with his shirt.

She hands him a napkin with a frown. "Nope, everything's squared away. I'll finish up the afternoon tasks, no problem."

"Thank you." Apollo grins before turning to me. "That grey Accord out there yours?"

"Yes. The application said delivering orders was part of the job?"

"That's correct. So, I have a quick"—he coughs—"call to make, but please meet me by your car in half an hour. The time in-between is all for you."

I nod and enjoy more pizza as Freddie chuckles, sipping her iced tea. Apollo excuses himself and retreats inside to his tiny office.

2:11 says the Accord clock when Len Apollo, sunglasses back on, leaves the office and enthrones himself in my passenger seat.

Looks like his "business call" with Sour Diesel and Pineapple Express went swimmingly.

"So, where are we going?" I ask, trying to hide my nerves and sound brave as we pass the Found Farms sign.

He's taking me somewhere secluded to kill me, hang me up, and sell my carcass at the farm as ethically-sourced jerky.

"Just down the road," rasps Apollo. He's not fooling me as he tries to talk while his lungs frantically re-oxygenate. "Speaking of day trading earlier, what are you investing in nowadays?"

"I don't care to invest," I say, keeping my eyes on the road with both hands on the wheel. "I wouldn't even know where to start," I admit.

"Oh, we'll do something about that," Apollo says,

looking out the window, lost in thought for only a moment before telling me to take a left.

"I mean right!" he yells before chuckling at himself.

One left, then jerked-right turn later, we end up at a small hiking trail.

Where the fuck is he taking me? SCAM ALERT SCAM ALERT. I'm pinning my location.

"We're not going far," Apollo says while basking in the September sun, freeing another button from his shirt to reveal more chest beard. If I didn't know any better, I'd think I was witnessing a human undergoing photosynthesis.

"Just over here," he says as he starts walking. Just a few yards from where I parked, he takes me to a shaded grove of trees.

Ok, here's where the money is buried. Maybe drugs! No, this is where I'm hacked up into pieces.

While I'm grasping my phone in my pocket just in case, I can't help but see this through. For a man without a single muscle or idea—let alone a clue—going out absurd like this will at least make for a great headline.

But instead of a poison dart hitting my neck or some dudes in camouflage coming out with a rice sack to throw over my head, I smell something pleasant that I never have before. For a second, I imagine its what chloroform smells like right before you go down.

Instead, it's sort of a sweet, tropical aroma. As we get closer to the trees, so does the scent flooding my nose. And before I know it, I'm under thirty-five-foot-high trees with the same teardrop leaves from before. But this time, I discover odd green fruits that look like unripe avocados hanging from the branches.

"Dino, these are pawpaw trees. Ever heard of them?" Apollo asks me.

"Like in the Jungle Book?" I ask back.

"No. But that's a different story," he says laughing.

"So what are they?" I ask.

"Asimina triloba is the name, being the most awesome fruit in America's the game," he quips.

"So why are we here?" I ask.

"See, my new hire, after I got into gardening, I started looking into fruits and vegetables I had never heard of before." he says.

He's starting another tale, I think to myself. Grabbing fruit from a low-hanging branch, he opens it up to reveal a soft, creamy, almost custard-like pulp with rows of large black seeds. Then he looks at the trees.

"I learned of these beauties right when they were in season. I spend days on end in the woods around here, hoping to find a patch. Luckily, I managed to find these before I got a tick bite."

"I see. So what is it?" I ask.

"It's a tropical fruit that survived the last Ice Age and has been growing here in our backyards well before people were even here." Apollo says, smirking, amused by my way of questioning.

I've never heard of this fruit before, yet here it is right in front of me, not thirty minutes away from my childhood home. I'm a man left in awe.

"The original people of this great continent, as

well as the early American settlers and early U.S. Presidents, all loved this fruit." He picks up another fruit from the ground. "Even their slaves," he says, finishing his thought with something between somber and rage.

At this point, I've taken my own pawpaw from a branch and split the fruit open with my hands just like Apollo. It's a little softer than a ripe avocado, and I can't help but smell the tropical goodness that's coming out of this unassuming Buss Ass trail.

"Then around the twentieth century, grocery stores started popping up, and the pawpaw fell into woodland obscurity. They don't ship well or have a good shelf life."

He's clearly reveling in reciting this story.

"That is, until the 1970s, when a guy as resplendent as ourselves tamed the pawpaw." He says, winking something cheesy. "Now, there's a small but dedicated pawpaw following across the world."

"What's so different about the tamed ones?" I ask.

"The cultivated ones are easily twice or thrice the size of these ones," he says.

"Really?" I ask with a raised eyebrow.

"We're talking one- to two-pounders, easy," he says with his perhaps nine-hundredth smirk today.

"Interesting..." I manage to say, taking in much more than I was expecting on my first day.

"Try it. Here's how." Apollo says.

He opens another. Avoiding the skin and seeds, he starts sucking the pulp from the fruit in his hands. He looks like a madman doing it, but naturally, I follow suit.

And wow... the taste... is all my scam meter can read.

I can't put my finger on it. It's like a banana; but mango; but pineapple. Maybe citrus or melon? Such a complex and delicious taste, a texture almost like custard. Meanwhile, pawpaw pulp is all over Apollo's five-o'clock shadow and the sunglasses on his chest.

"You like 'em?" Apollo asks, spitting large black seeds into the air like a rain of bullets.

"I do. I feel like this would be a great substitute for anything using bananas." I spit a seed out myself.

"I'm in the company of another man of fine taste!" he says, then nearly chokes on the last seed shooting from his mouth.

"I know a few people who think it tastes like semen," he adds, before laughing probably harder than I've seen him laugh today. And somehow, I am too.

"No fucking way?!" I say without even realizing it.

"No lie!" he says, now choking through his laughter.

I'm still looking at the trees, the fruit, and the seeds now littered all over this patch, and I'm reminded why we're here to begin with.

I'm Dino Toilston, and my question still hasn't been answered...

"Ok, so pawpaws are here, they've been here, they're amazing, and they have a niche cult following. But what's that have to do with funding the farm?"

Apollo grins at the question, his dimple making another cameo. In fact, he's grinning harder than I've ever seen him grin today, and that's been nearly a thousand times so far. In fact, this is the first time I've noticed the gold tooth on the front row near his molar.

"These babies sell for ten to fifteen dollars a pound,

easy. I didn't show you ours yet because I wanted to show you trees in their wild habitat first, but the farm has dozens upon dozens of pawpaw trees in that far back corner we avoided earlier."

"Ah!" I deduce, rolling my eyes at him.

"The trees you said weren't worth much."

"Hehe." Apollo grins. "And they're not trees that produce small, wild fruits like this."

He gestures to the pawpaw in his hand.

"We sell thousands of pounds of pawpaws a year, on top of their seeds, saplings, and everything else you've seen growing today."

He shows me a few more wild pawpaw trees in the area before we eventually head back to Found.

Returning to the farm, I admit this is not what I was expecting for the first day. Freddie greets us both at the door as we get out of the Accord. I notice the dash reads 4:23 before I pull the key from the ignition.

"So, how were the pawpaws?" Freddie asks Apollo.

"They're a little sweeter this year," he chirps, walking towards her while also turning his neck to me. "Whadjya think about them, Dino?"

"I'll be honest, I don't know what to say. I had no idea something so rich in history and taste could be growing right in front of our faces."

I decide to power down my scam meter for today.

"That's exactly what I thought when he first hired me!" says Winifred.

"Tomorrow, I'll teach you everything you need to

know about our pawpaws." He puffs his chest but then deflates, as if his battery has run dry. "But we can call it short today."

Before walking inside the office, he pats me on the back and smiles.

"Welcome to Found Farms."

Driving home, I pat a baggy of pulpy pawpaw seeds in my pocket and decide to plant them in my backyard when I get home. I can't help but think about what my parents are going to say about today. The shipping container office, the enigma of my new boss, Found's Garden-of-Eden farm, the golden cash cow that is the pawpaw.

My friends don't garden or have any fucking idea what a pawpaw is; I'll finally get to teach them something incredible for once.

And I almost forgot the cherry on top—I'm getting paid thirty-five dollars an hour with pizza perks.

Yeah, that recruiter can kiss my black ass.

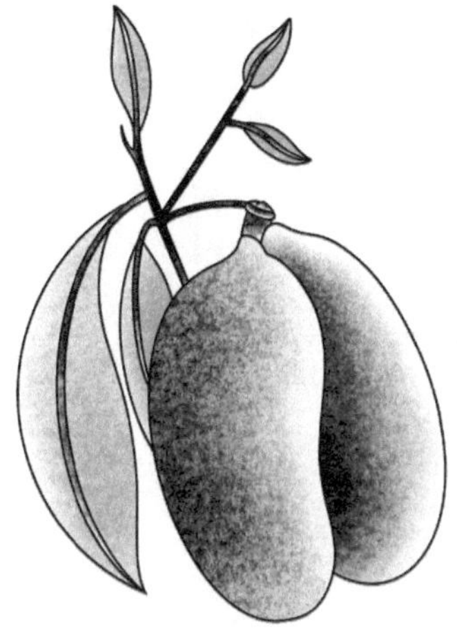

National Pawpaw Day
is the third Thursday of every September.

ABOUT THE AUTHOR

Leslie Summerfield is a DMV born and raised author/ poet whose writing style is yours to decide; as an esteemed peer once asked:

"What are you feeding your mind to write like this?"

Their work blends Black intellectual and liberation traditions, relatable yet raw, provocative humor, strange circumstance, and an obsessive love for the overlooked.

DID YOU ENJOY THIS BOOK?

Get the e-book, discover another TJP title, or follow our socials for more!

Come visit
Buss ~~Ask~~ **ASS**
Again Soon!

www.ingramcontent.com/pod-product-compliance
Lightning Source LLC
Chambersburg PA
CBHW051447140726
47987CB00006B/2579